WHY THIS IS AN EASY READER

- This story has been carefully written to keep the young reader's interest high.

- It is told in a simple, open style, with a strong rhythm that adds enjoyment both to reading aloud and silent reading.

- There is a very high percentage of words repeated. It is this skillful repetition which helps the child to read independently. Seeing words again and again, he "practices" the vocabulary he knows, and learns with ease the words that are new.

- Only 114 different words have been used, with plurals and root words counted once.

   48 words—over one-third the total vocabulary—are used at least three times.

   29 words—one-fourth the total vocabulary—are used at least five times.

   Some words have been used 15 and 23 times.

ABOUT THIS STORY

- Here is the extravagant humor beloved by the young school child, made even more enjoyable because it is built around the familiar problem of minding baby brother.

- The rhyming makes for special ease of reading and gives good practice in recognizing likenesses in sounds.

Billy Brown:
The Baby Sitter

Story by TAMARA KITT

Pictures by ROSALIND WELCHER

Editorial Consultant: LILIAN MOORE

WONDER BOOKS
A Division of Grosset & Dunlap, Inc.
New York, N.Y. 10010

Introduction

These books are meant to help the young reader discover what a delightful experience reading can be. The stories are such fun that they urge the child to try his new reading skills. They are so easy to read that they will encourage and strengthen him as a reader.

The adult will notice that the sentences aren't too long, the words aren't too hard, and the skillful repetition is like a helping hand. What the child will feel is: "This is a good story—and I can read it myself!"

For some children, the best way to meet these stories may be to hear them read aloud at first. Others, who are better prepared to read on their own, may need a little help in the beginning—help that is best given freely. Youngsters who have more experience in reading alone—whether in first or second or third grade—will have the immediate joy of reading "all by myself."

These books have been planned to help all young readers grow—in their pleasure in books and in their power to read them.

Lilian Moore
Specialist in Reading
Formerly of Division of Instructional Research,
New York City Board of Education

"Billy, Billy, will you do

Something that I want you to?"

"Yes, Ma. You know I like to do Something that surprises you."

"Oh! No surprises! No, indeed!
Surprises are not what I need."

"Billy, tell me you will do
What I am going to ask of you."

"OK, Ma. OK, OK.

I'll do anything you say."

"Then here is the baby,
Billy Brown.
Take care of him while I go
to town."

"Oh no, Ma, no!

Ma, please don't go."

"Or, if you do,

Then take him, too."

"I cannot take him with me.
I have to go to town."

"So stop that silly talking.

Take him walking, Billy Brown!"

"By-by, Baby. Say good-by
to your mother.
You will have lots of fun
with your brother."

"It's no fun. It's no fun.
Ma, I like to play and run!"

"Now, Billy! Not another peep out of you."

"The baby soon will fall asleep.

Googly-goo."

"Googly-goo and googly-ga.

Why can't you go with our Ma?"

"OK, Googly, want some fun?

I will take you for a run!"

"Googly, googly, run, run, run!

Boy oh boy! Say, this is fun!"

"Billy! Don't run
    with your brother!
I am going to
    tell your mother!"

"Look out! A bee! Here comes another!"

"Oh, Billy, Billy, where's your
brother?"

"Billy, Billy! Get him! Get him!
Billy, Billy! Do not let him
get away!"

"I will get him! I will get him!
No, no, no! I will not let him
    get away!"

"Look out! Look out!"

"Don't yell at me!
The baby's sleeping.
Can't you see?"

"No, but I see something now.
Billy, look! Look, Billy!"

"WOW!"

"Billy, Billy, run, run, run!"

"Boy, oh boy! Say, this is fun!"

"Fun, is it? Where are we? Stop!"

"We are here, way up on top."

"Billy! Help!"

"Don't yell! Don't yell!
The baby's sleeping.
Can't you tell?"

"Oh, my goodness, Billy Brown!

Tell the man to put us down!"

"Please put us down.

Down! Down! I say!"

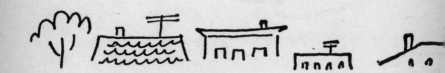

"Oh, my goodness, Billy Brown,
I am glad that we are down.
How is your brother?
Where's your mother?"

"She is coming back from town."

"Billy, Billy,

How's your brother?"

"Hello, Baby.

Come to Mother."

"Tell me, Billy,

Can you say—

Did the baby

Sleep OK?"

"Oh yes, Ma."

"Tell me, Baby,

Is that true?"

"Googly, Mama,

Googly-goo."

CHOOSE FROM THESE EASY READERS

5901 Will You Come to My Party?
5902 Hurry Up, Slowpoke
5903 Mr. Pine's Mixed-up Signs
5904 The Adventures of Silly Billy
5905 The Secret Cat
5906 Billy Brown Makes Something Grand
5907 Miss Polly's Animal School
5908 The Duck on the Truck
5909 A Train for Tommy
5910 Surprise in the Tree
5911 The Monkey in the Rocket
5912 Billy Brown: The Baby Sitter
5913 Fly-Away at the Air Show
5914 Arty the Smarty
5915 The Surprising Pets of Billy Brown
5916 Barney Beagle
5917 I Made a Line
5918 Laurie and the Yellow Curtains
5919 Grandpa's Wonderful Glass
5920 Benjamin in the Woods
5921 Barney Beagle Plays Baseball
5922 The Day Joe Went to the Supermarket
5923 Question and Answer Book
5924 Jokes and Riddles
5925 Let Papa Sleep!
5926 The Surprise in the Story Book
5927 The Big Green Thing
5928 The Boy Who Fooled the Giant
5929 More Jokes and Riddles
5930 Too Many Pockets
5931 The Clumsy Cowboy
5932 Cat in the Box
5933 How the Animals Get to the Zoo
5934 The Birthday Party
5935 Little Gray Mouse and the Train